PRAISE FOR M. L. BUCHMAN

Top 10 Romance of 2012, 2015, and 2016.

— AMERICAN LIBRARY ASSOCIATION'S *BOOKLIST:* THE NIGHT IS MINE, HOT POINT, HEART STRIKE

One of our favorite authors.

— RT BOOK REVIEWS

Buchman has catapulted his way to the top tier of my favorite authors.

— FRESH FICTION

A favorite author of mine. I'll read anything that carries his name, no questions asked. Meet your new favorite author!

— THE SASSY BOOKSTER, FLASH OF FIRE

M.L. Buchman is guaranteed to get me lost in a good story.

— THE READING CAFE, WAY OF THE
WARRIOR: NSDQ

I love Buchman's writing. His vivid descriptions bring everything to life in an unforgettable way.

— PURE JONEL, HOT POINT

MIRROR-MOON LIGHT, MIRROR-MOON BRIGHT

A FUTURE NIGHT STALKERS 2352 A.D. ROMANCE STORY

M. L. BUCHMAN

Buchman Bookworks

Other works by M. L. Buchman:

The Night Stalkers

MAIN FLIGHT
The Night Is Mine
I Own the Dawn
Wait Until Dark
Take Over at Midnight
Light Up the Night
Bring On the Dusk
By Break of Day

WHITE HOUSE HOLIDAY
Daniel's Christmas
Frank's Independence Day
Peter's Christmas
Zachary's Christmas
Roy's Independence Day
Damien's Christmas

AND THE NAVY
Christmas at Steel Beach
Christmas at Peleliu Cove

5E
Target of the Heart
Target Lock on Love
Target of Mine

Firehawks

MAIN FLIGHT
Pure Heat
Full Blaze
Hot Point
Flash of Fire
Wild Fire

SMOKEJUMPERS
Wildfire at Dawn
Wildfire at Larch Creek
Wildfire on the Skagit

Delta Force
Target Engaged
Heart Strike
Wild Justice

White House Protection Force
Off the Leash
On Your Mark
In the Weeds

Where Dreams
Where Dreams are Born
Where Dreams Reside
Where Dreams Are of Christmas
Where Dreams Unfold
Where Dreams Are Written

Eagle Cove
Return to Eagle Cove
Recipe for Eagle Cove
Longing for Eagle Cove
Keepsake for Eagle Cove

Henderson's Ranch
Nathan's Big Sky
Big Sky, Loyal Heart

Love Abroad
Heart of the Cotswolds: England
Path of Love: Cinque Terre, Italy

Dead Chef Thrillers
Swap Out!
One Chef!
Two Chef!

Deities Anonymous
Cookbook from Hell: Reheated
Saviors 101

SF/F Titles
The Nara Reaction
Monk's Maze
the Me and Elsie Chronicles

Strategies for Success (NF)
Managing Your Inner Artist/Writer
Estate Planning for Authors

"You did not just do that to me! I'll launch you out the nearest airlock if I have to get a Plas torch and cut a new one myself."

Colonel Deeton just shrugged. He knew her threats were empty, damn him, but she was seriously tempted this time.

"You saddled me with a rook?"

"He's not a rookie."

She glanced through the window at the dweeb seated front and center outside Deeton's cube. Then she rolled her eyes back to her commander. "He's got first-stage rook written all over him."

"No, he doesn't, Syra" Deeton scrubbed at his graying beard as he always did when she was irritating him. "He's got *engineer* written all over him."

"Oh, like that's any kind of an improvement."

"Full payload." Meaning he was the real deal no matter how he looked.

At least it explained a few things, though not enough of them. He was an engineer who looked like a rook, yet he looked like a soldier not a dweeb engineer. Workout shoulders. She'd always been partial to shoulders on her soldiers. "Oh, like a rook dweeb *engineer* is so much better than a rook dweeb *soldier*."

"Got all the soldier we need right here if she weren't running off at the mouth so hard." Deeton tossed a chip at her. "Won't unlock until you're clear of the station."

She let it ping off the window behind her before she caught it on the rebound. No hurry in low-g. It was eye-dent sealed *and* station locked. Her kind of mission.

"Whose eye?"

This time it was Deeton's turn to roll *his* remaining eye at *her*—the other had gone the way of half his face sometime during the Drone Downfall. He didn't talk about it much.

The eye-dent required *her* retinal scan, of course.

"It was a gimme, Deet," she explained when he didn't rise to the bait. "Just feeling sorry for you playing two legs short of a full deck." The Drone Downfall had been ugly.

The Drone Downfall still ranked as the most lethal undeclared war in history (which was saying something serious).

You broke my heart, and then an untraceable Class II drone slams through the windshield of your skidder at Mach 2.

I deserved a raise, revenged by calling in sick and delivering five kilos of Hydrox rocket fuel and a sparker to the office by remotely controlled drone. Politicos who hadn't bunkered, and bunkered deep, didn't last long back then.

The I-Loc, International Law of Control, had required trackable human control via DNA scan of every drone flying. The same had been required on every computer with an intelligence above Level Four— it was the last thing the countries of Earth and Near Space had been able to agree on. The remaining government of Canmerica West had taken it upon themselves to take out all non-complying drones— Canmerica East had long since stopped being a factor. And it was fliers like Deeton who'd taken the abuse.

Letting the chip ricochet off the window had also given her an excuse to eye the RDE again. A severe regressive: blond hair and blue eyes—neither looked fake. Nor did the smile as his gaze met hers through the window.

"What's the lowdown on it, Colonel?"

"The lowdown, Syra? I don't have a scope on it. They didn't tell me anything but to get our very best on it."

"Aw, shucks."

"Since Daggert isn't available, I'm stuck with you."

"Daggert can barely find his own back end to wipe it."

"Whereas you're all brown from sticking your nose in it. Get out of my space, Syra. Try not to embarrass the fleet while you're at it."

"Shit," she kicked open the door and walked out past the RDE. "Come on, Rood, you're with me." Rood

—Rook Dweeb. She liked it. Maybe she could make it stick on the guy.

"Shouldn't that be Roodee—Rook Dweeb Engineer. Like a roadie. Or maybe the final 'e' sound is silent," he rose to his feet a little fast and floated up off the floor in the light grav. *For crap's sake!*

"What's a roadie?" He wasn't supposed to have heard what she was saying in Deet's office. Could she help it if her voice carried when Deet was making her nutsoid?

"Old days. Guy who traveled with bands to set up their gear for a show."

"Not just a regressive," she kept moving but noticed that he didn't react. "Regressive" was not a kind label.

She'd have beat the O2 out of someone who called her that.

"A retro one," which compensated a bit as there was a coolness to it that she'd never achieved.

Though what a band of soldiers needed with a roadie was beyond her. She'd humped her own gear for her entire service. For her entire life. Mom had been hunting this deck long before she had. Keeping the Royal Delta Marines at the top of the military heap was a hereditary job as well as a chosen one.

Grandmom had fought for Canmerica all the way back before it divided into East and West—that's how long the Clairborne women had been fighting the good fight.

Syra dropped downshaft to null-g then had to wait while Rood hung onto a slider. Below two-gees, slider handles were strictly for civilians. No self-respecting human used one for the transition from one-quarter at command levels down to zero at the docks.

Rood did. And was sweating by the time she grabbed him. If she hadn't, he might have hung onto the slider right back up the opposite axis—which could cause real problems if you entered the shaft feet first through the gravity flip. Good way to break something permanent, like your neck.

"Where did you come from, Rood? Earth?"

He looked a little green as he nodded. She hadn't met one of those in a long while. Earthers were as rare as blonds with blue eyes. Maybe that's all that was left down there.

"You spew on me, Rood, and we're gonna have issues. Clear?"

He nodded again and clamped his jaw harder.

She dug into her med kit, found a patch in a little used corner, and slapped it on his neck. "Close your eyes and count to ten."

She inspected him while she waited. He was tall for a full-grav grounder—almost her height. Spacer-borns added ten or twenty centimeters just for not living in brutal Earth grav every damn minute of the day. And he had a layer of muscle that even the toughest Marine couldn't lay on because it simply wasn't natural in space. Spacers were long and lean unless they were some civvie who lived their whole life in the outermost level of a rotating habitat can—and what kind of life was that?

His suit was a standard c-fiber rig, so knock off a few centimeters breadth on those nice shoulders, but still majorly brawny. Not bad looking once she got used to the blond hair, which was gonna take a while.

Surreal though, when he opened those weirdly blue eyes—who knew what he could see with those. Almost made her check that she wore a full suit and wasn't standing there in just her skin. Like he could see right inside her.

He looked more stable now though. She didn't tell him about the lockjaw that wouldn't wear off for a couple of minutes.

If all Royal Delta Marines looked like her, he'd sign up tomorrow. Lucius had never actually met a RDM before. The old Canmerican Delta Force had merged with the British Royal Marines a quarter century back when Canmerica had finally gone down hard. The Deltas and the Night Stalkers—Canmerica's elite fighters and fliers—had fought their way out to orbit and the Brits had given them a home.

Syra looked half cat and half invisible in her skin-tight black jumpsuit. He didn't see a spare gram anywhere, but rumor said that an RDM could step out an airlock and complete any mission with just what they were wearing.

Smoothly bald. Rumor was they all shaved their heads to save the extra ounces. Of course so did half of spacers—hair and zero-g he supposed could be awkward. His own seemed to be okay, but he'd never worn it long. Bald looked silly on some women, but not her.

"Am I going to like what's on this chip?" She led him into a hangar that looked like a rabbit warren for ships. A line of the big Stinger 60s of the Night Stalkers filled one side of the bay. The other side of the hangar housed a long rack of smaller vessels. In the ceiling racks were parked all of the utility craft, and the floor area was service bays and gear. She led him to one that had to be too small for human use. It wasn't just space black. It was so black that it hurt his eyes trying to see it.

"Hm-nmn. Nmnnm." Something was wrong with his mouth. He was starting to panic when he caught her hints of a sly grin.

He managed a calming breath, then poked her shoulder to get her to turn to fully face him. It was weird, she was hard, like Plas hard. He was fairly sure he'd know if they'd figured out android bodies.

"Mn rm nu?"

"What am I? An RDM. So don't screw with me. It'll wear off in a few minutes." Her smile was a good one. He didn't have a whole lot of experience with women, though he suspected that any experience he did have wouldn't have been relevant with a Marine anyway.

She rested her hand against the impenetrable darkness of the small ship and a hatch appeared. An Insertion Ship. He'd heard of these, mostly by rumor. They were the next an extreme evolution from the Bell Little Bird attack helicopter—the same way humans were to whatever proceeded chimpanzees. It was little bigger and could carry just two people, but that's where the similarities ended. Canmerica, while they still existed, and now the Brits knew one thing—give your Special Ops teams the very best gear. Inserters were almost mythic in their capabilities. Stealth, weapons, and computers that were so smart they were barely legal even with I-Loc control by humans.

The engineer in him wanted a full rundown. One look at Syra told him to keep his mouth shut even if he could talk.

At her gesture, he entered first. The first seat was beyond crazy. It made the cockpit of the Earth Launch ship look like a surface slider's control panel in comparison. The second seat was devoid of controls—a half dozen interfaces that he recognized and not much more. He opted for that one. There was no third seat— not as if there was room for one.

His ears popped after she slid in and closed the hatch. A quick run of her hands over the controls, and the ship seemed to wake to life. A thumb on the I-LoC pad and the computer came online.

She slotted the chip.

"Id wond murk mile dockd."

"This ship has a few tricks that aren't on the books." She punched some control. "Poof! We're no longer here. But we are. But we aren't. You wanna tell me about what's on here before I crack it?"

"I can't!" He wanted to yell it in exasperation, and somehow he could.

Her smile again looked dangerous. Pretty as hell, but dangerous. An RDM with dimples. He wondered what color her hair really was that went with those curiously green eyes. Even rarer than his own blue.

"I…" he tried in a normal voice, and it worked. "We're going to steal something."

She shrugged, "Fine by me."

Oddly, her Plas-hard suit seemed to flow with her underlying musculature. Armor wasn't one of his specialties, but he had no idea how she felt so hard yet looked so soft. Was the woman inside the armor like that as well?

"What are we stealing? And why you?" She was all business.

"Why me?" No one had asked him that. Up until this point, he'd explained what he'd figured out and then he'd been told "You're it!"

He had to think before he could answer the question.

"I suppose that it's because I'm the one who figured out how to steal it. As to what, maybe you'd better open the chip. I don't think it's likely that you'll believe me. I'm just a Rook Dweeb Engineer."

No smile at his joke, granted, lame joke. Not even a twitch that he could detect. She simply leaned down and eye-dented the chip. Maybe her brain was as hard as her armor. And her heart as cold and dark. But that wasn't right. He'd heard her fiery temper when she'd unleashed it on Colonel Deeton. Everyone had, despite the closed door.

He'd built the main infrastructure of the chip's contents. The Royal Delta Marines commander-in-chief had been the one to lay in the mission orders and lock it down.

"Royal Engineer Lucius Markham…" the commander's voice sounded into the tiny cockpit.

"Even you name is retro," Syra muttered.

"…is in absolute and unquestioned command of this mission. Acknowledge."

"What kind of space junk is that?" Syra yelled at the commander.

But he was a recording, only programmed to respond to one answer.

"Acknowledge," the chip responded. "Message will autodestruct in ten. Nine. Eight…"

Lucius could hear her teeth grinding. At Two, she snapped out. "Acknowledge. Major Syra Clairborne of the Royal Delta Marines."

"Acknowledge accepted," the chip answered flatly.

Her fury seemed to seethe off her in waves that threatened to flood the tiny cockpit.

"Major Syra Clairborne? You're *that* Syra?" She had a reputation that carried all the way to Earth. A lethal one. She was the most decorated soldier of them all.

His question gave her a focus for her irritation. If looks were lethal…

He raised his hands. "Not my idea. Please don't kill me."

3

"Tempting, but no." Because the Rook Dweeb Engineer was the one in command.

Killing a superior officer—even a temporary one who might deserve it—was outside even *her* typical fast-and-loose get-it-done-and-explain-later tactic.

"You're not even military. What tight orbit do you have on the commander's personal exhaust port that he did that?"

"Personal exhaust por…"

"Whatever you call an asshole on Earth."

"We, uh, call it an asshole."

She just grunted at the foolishness of that, but could feel a slip of a smile trying to form even though she ordered it to stay hidden. The guy wasn't just cute, he was definitely an engineer through and through. They always had to understand everything as they went along. RDMs learned to make it up as they went.

"I think," he seemed to be inspecting the ceiling. His

hair shifted so lightly and easily. If she had hair like that, she might wear it long—even if it was blond. "It's because the required methods of success are extremely specific. He wanted to make sure that you didn't try to countermand them. There's only one way in."

She didn't like his mindreading trick either. Telepathy was still all debris-field, but it unnerved her anyway.

"Target?" she snarled at the eye-dent chip for lack of a better victim. Syra hoped that her on-board comp caught that she was yelling at the chip and not her. Star—technically called Strategic-Tactical Analysis and Response computer by unimaginative people like engineers who actually called her Starc—got sulky when Syra yelled at her. But Syra'd be spaced before she'd ask some civilian "commander" for anything.

In answer, a hologram unfolded between them. It built layer by layer from the inside, rather than simply flashing up. The sheer volume of data that implied was a little humbling. Normally Star would be able to interpret it in a single gestalt.

Once the complexities of the inner structure expanded, the outer structure began taking shape. It wasn't just the complexity, it was the sheer scale of it.

Something was definitely wrong with her suit. The recirc and process layer fit her like a second skin. In many ways it *was* a second skin: controlling temperature, moisture, and chemical balance into a steady state from inside the habitat to floating in open space. It also fed biometrics alerts. If her helmet was on, they'd probably be flashing her blind. Heart palpitations. Cold sweat on her palms and forehead. If her hands ever shook, they'd be shaking.

"I did not sign up to die," she managed to keep her voice steady.

"Me either."

"But…" she could only point.

"The Mirror Moon, as the India Beam reflector is colloquially called, is held in a geostationary orbit at an altitude of only five hundred kilometers." The fuel expenditure to do that had always been mind warping. Geostationary was another thirty-five thousand klicks up the grav well.

"It's too well protected, we've never been able to destroy it." Syra could only glare at the thing that made every ship's life pure hell.

It had to be the best offense system ever devised—it was the upper point of the India Particle Beam. No one, in or out of their right mind, entered that sector of space, or any sector for a long way around.

Most economies had launched into space as the Earth became less and less viable as a biome. The Brits had built a whole chain of habitat cans at Lagrange 2 above the Lunar Farside. They might be in the "asshole of space" but it was one of the best strategic locales in all Earth orbit—nothing done from Earth, by India or anyone else, could reach them here behind the moon. Once Canmerica West had abruptly collapsed as thoroughly as East, the remaining military forces had fought their way into orbit. Delta Force had joined the Royal Marines and the Night Stalkers had just kept doing what they did—delivering Special Operations teams any time, any where…and getting their asses back out afterward.

The Aussies and Kiwis had stayed on the surface, but had come up with the best *defense* system ever. The Aussies had thrown up a force dome that nothing penetrated. Certainly nothing human-made. The eggheads had determined that fish, waves, and wind went through, but not even a guy in a rowboat made it in. Just a flash and all that was left was a puff of molecular components. Even seeing it, no one could figure how it had been done. One day, after a lot of constant begging by the Kiwis, the dome had suddenly extended to encompass New Zealand. Now that they'd truly gone Down Under, none of DUs were saying how it worked. They might as well not be on the face of the Earth any longer.

India, confronted with how to move its five billion into space with almost no resources, had come up with a different solution for national security. They had launched a vast reflector into space—without anyone quite knowing what they were up to. Solar power harvesting didn't need such a device anymore, but with the Indian way of thinking, it was impossible to tell what they were up to until it was too late.

India had explained the kilometer-wide reflector's purpose on a Thursday morning with a clear demonstration. They unleashed a massive particle beam that had punched upward from an underground complex deep in the peaks and ridges of the Western Ghats.

From its height in orbit, the mirror had redirected

the beam back down to the surface at an angle. With a strategic horizon of twenty-five hundred kilometers at the mirror's altitude, the Indians had laid down a thousand kilometers of scorched earth in every direction past their borders. The Saudis, Iranians, Afghanis, and especially the Pakistanis weren't going to bother anyone ever again. The Nepalese, and a wide swath from Bangladesh to Myanmar weren't going to say much ever again either.

That single, massive energy expenditure had caused a minor ice age across the Ghats and the terawatts of heat retransferred had finally tipped the balance on the polar ice, drowning all of India's coastal cities from Mumbai to Calcutta as Antarctica and Greenland mostly disappeared beneath the rising ocean. Between the descending ice and the catastrophic ocean rise, there were now closer to two billion Indians rather than five. Up in orbit, there was much debate about whether or not that might have been part of the plan—down on Earth, no one was saying.

But still the India Particle Beam and the IPB Reflector (the Mirror Moon) dominated the entire hemisphere. And while even the Indians weren't likely to fire off another major burst, they weren't above minor bursts to make sure no flights entered most of the Earth's Eastern hemisphere.

Syra finally absorbed the implications of the mission. Without the Mirror Moon, the particle beam's effective reach would shrink to a narrow cone of space little bigger than India itself. For those still on Earth, it wouldn't merely be a boon to navigation, it was a matter of survival to get off the surface.

"You can do that? Destroy the Mirror Moon?" Not many people awed her. Colonel Deeton was one, though she'd never let him know that. But if the Roodee could pull that off, Lucius Markham could be making a fast jump into that category.

But he shook his head.

"*What?* Then what are we doing here?"

"Where's the fun in destroying it when we can steal it?"

"Steal it?" Syra just shook her head. What was wrong with this guy? "I get that your name means light, but…well…damn, Lucius. And don't forget all of the control systems on the back of that thing; they mass way more than the mirror. Where are you going to hide a kilometer-across mirror?"

"That's for me to know and them to never find out. They'll never see it again where we're headed." Then he smiled.

She knew that smile. It was the same one she saw in a mirror just before a mission.

He might be a Rook Dweeb Engineer, but he was her kind of Roodee.

She released the computer. She didn't have to tell Star anything. Star had long since learned that when Syra released the controls, it meant "Go. Now."

They went. And she wondered what else the RDE wasn't so dweeby about.

4

Lucius hadn't really thought through the next part of the mission. Actually, he had. He simply hadn't calculated on spending it with Major Syra Clairborne in the close confines of an Inserter ship.

"India has one blind spot," he'd explained. "The sun is pouring out more than 1.367 kilowatts per square meter per hour. If we come directly out of the sun, timed to when the Mirror Moon exactly aligns in orbit with the sun, we should be undetectable among the 4.29 gigawatts of solar energy pouring down on the satellite's solar collector."

"How far out?"

Syra's question had led to a debate on just how invisible an Inserter was. Once he'd done the math, it simply felt too close. So they'd looped out an extra ten million kilometers. Syra even had the idea of staying off-axis and waiting an extra day for the Earth's orbit to swing into alignment with them, rather than making a maneuver right in front of the sun. They'd look like little more than some lazily wandering space rock in visible light—they wouldn't leave the slightest trace on radar due to the Inserter's stealth design. Also, with the sun behind them, their engine's heat would also be invisible.

That was all good.

But it had meant most of three days living side by side with Syra and Star in the tiny Inserter. Zero-g meant that sleeping aboard the ship wasn't a problem. And the suits were comfortable enough that it didn't matter that there wasn't room to take them off.

Star herself was interesting. He enjoyed their three-way discussions. He'd worked with AIs before—incredibly advanced calculating ones anyway. But Star was advanced enough to have what passed for opinions of her own. Sometimes she and Syra would squabble over minor points. He half wondered if Syra had programmed her computer to do that—she certainly seemed to enjoy the debate.

Syra herself was a different matter. She attacked everything. Every idea he put forth, she dove into wholeheartedly and gleefully shredded it to the winds. His own habits—methodically building a hypothesis and working to layer on credible evidence then test for structural flaws to the expanding solution—survived bare seconds beneath her barrage.

"No. No. No. The Chinese and Canmerica West were never going to survive in space together no matter how you contrived it."

"But if they had cooperated to—"

"The last time they cooperated was when the old

Canmerica Combined allowed their economy to be shredded by Chinese imports. Who built the L5 Habitat cans for Canmerica?"

She didn't even give him time to answer.

"The Chinese. So how did the Chinese solve the final trade war? They switched off the environmental systems that the Canmericans had hired them to run."

"But—"

"Right." Syra was on a roll and there was no stopping her. "The Canmericans weren't idiots, but they were never subtle. The Chinese were ready for anything from the Canmericans, except brute force. They expected and prepared for computer viruses or even a missile. They didn't expect a doomsday command that launched a two hundred kilometer-wide asteroid into their hab-can's orbital path three months later—long after they'd let their guard down." The asteroid was so vast it had barely noticed wiping out the massive Chinese orbital complex.

"I always assumed that the Brits did that."

Syra's puzzled look surprised him. Making her racing thought processes screech to halt for even a moment made him want to laugh.

"Because of the asteroid's name. The one they used to erase the Chinese from orbit."

Still nothing.

"Asteroid 121 has the common name of Hermione."

That led him to trying to explain pre-space literature to someone who never read fiction.

"What did your mother read you at bedtime, the Royal Delta Marine training manuls?"

"Yes." Syra's tone said he was being stupid to even ask.

He had no good answer to that.

He also had no good answer to how he was feeling about Syra Clairborne. She was stubborn, driven, opinionated, dangerous, and if he was a different man—with no particular fear of dying—he'd have grabbed her by the end of Day Two and seen just what could be done in the tiny confines of an Inserter.

Of course, he'd have to ask Star to shut down her inputs.

5

Star's biometrics registration system monitored her passengers' health and well being in addition to the ship's mechanical status, and any external threats from wandering asteroids to dust particle impacts.

Her circuits were unsure how to interpret the new inputs.

Syra Clairborne's biometrics were ingrained on her memory banks as deeply as her own core processor temperatures. Every state and pattern known and instantly recognizable. Sleeping, digesting, full battle, even bleeding out and requiring immediate intervention. Those Star knew.

But she was puzzled by her current readings of Syra; as puzzled as an AI could be.

Higher than average body heat, invariant with cabin ambient.

Pupils dilated excessively for lumens setting.

A laugh. It was so unusual, Star had to open up a

backlink against orders to verify that's what it actually was. But it compared with a 97.4 percent commonality with the ten thousand samples she pulled over the Interwave—98.6 percent correlation when compared with the limited sample available of Royal Delta Marines.

That led her to waiting for Syra to perform a waste elimination into her suit's processing system and extracting a DNA match. Confirmed. Syra Clairborne was still Syra Clairborne.

Star inspected the non-communication interdiction order on the eye-dent chip. It did preclude contacting command for anything short of mental or physical incapacity. She weighed that against her own curiosity index settings regarding the changes in her partner.

Syra had stated on the first day that they were partners.

Star had monitored several thousand hours of information on "partners," ranging from Sam Spade forsaking the woman he loved because she killed his partner (one step too far in *The Maltese Falcon*) to Syra's own essay on team dynamics during her RDM training.

Star's conclusion was that while she had greater latitude to act than most other ships, there was also a high correlation factor between "partner" and "trust." As she was the former, it implied she should act equally strongly upon the latter. While not axiomatic upon inspection, it registered against her databanks as if it was anyway. For now, she would withhold judgment on Syra's inexplicable changes and simply "trust."

She considered analyzing the cabin's other

occupant, but Earthside links necessary to research Lucius Markham background data for baseline calculation registered too high a risk factor—at present. A quick review of her own functionality found a higher than expected weighting of internal processor load dedicated to answering his various queries.

Star didn't restore that weighted processing pathway to standard parameters, as his thoughts *were* interesting —when Syra wasn't shouting them out of existence. But Star did set an alarm circuit to notify her if her own dynamically-allocated capacity dedicated to the engineer Lucius Markham increased sufficiently to impede other processing tasks.

6

Syra knew something was wrong, but no matter how she searched Star's systems, she couldn't find anything the matter. Other than running basic diagnostics, she'd couldn't delve too deeply because Lucius sat close beside her and would want to know what was wrong. So she did her best to make it look like routine maintenance checks, which she never had to do because Star typically reported any systems' problem long before Syra could have detected them.

Star's latest diagnostic report ran one line longer than normal. It caught her attention simply because it wasn't in the normal pattern. The line displayed for such a short moment that Syra would have doubted it had been there, except for the latent impression on her retina:

It's not me.

If whatever was wrong wasn't Star…

Syra didn't like the implications of that, but couldn't ask the computer what she'd meant. Not with Lucius right there.

Everything looked normal.

Except for the looming Mirror Moon. It was finally expanding from a navigation point to displaying a visible diameter. At their current rate of closure, it would eclipse the Earth in another minute. They'd be aboard in two.

If the defense system didn't decide to kill them.

The mirror moon was a double mirror.

Facing Earth was a kilometer-wide reflector tuned to redirect and spread the ground-based particle beam into a lethal swath fifty-kilometers across. The Indians had raked it methodically over all of the surrounding landscape. They'd swept it over Pakistan for four complete passes. Not even microbes could have survived that level of abuse.

Facing the sun were a thousand steerable mirrors that had the opposite function: they gathered all of the sunlight striking the backside for the half orbit that it faced the sun. That sunlight was then focused on a collector tower at the very center of the mirror. That's where the Mirror Moon gathered the power to remain in a geosynchronous position despite being in Low Earth Orbit. It set up a magnetic field that pushed against Earth's magnetic field to keep it high above India.

Atop that solar energy collection tower was a flat spot too small for any ship…except an Inserter.

Hoping her retro rocket flare to land on the

collector's tip would be hidden by the sunlight pounding into the underside of the collector's head, Syra unleashed a full burn at the last second.

Star even calculated the maximum compression on her landing struts to minimize burn time. They slammed down, eliciting a hard grunt from Lucius. Then Star pinned them in place with maneuvering thrusters followed up with spikes ejected through the landing pads.

"Now what Mr. Genius Roodee?"

"Now we wait six hours."

"Why six hours?"

"Because thirty meters below us is the collection point for 4.29 gigawatts of solar energy. I'd rather not descend through that while the mirror is facing the sun."

Syra wondered at his calm. They were perched atop the deadliest weapon in Earth's very deadly history. Yet, they were oddly safe. Six hours with nothing to do except stare at the stars.

Nothing to do except listen to her pulse pounding in her ears.

"You know…" Lucius started in a soft voice, but his words ran out.

She knew. Her *body* knew. The Royal Dweeb Engineer had landed her on the ultimate target for a military operator. How many late nights had she spent in a Marine bar with a dozen other grunts trying to solve the Mirror Moon problem? Every scenario had been proposed: massive invasion forces (except Spec Ops was never a massive force, even before all of the disasters down on the surface), a small operational detachment (but they'd tried that and lost four top operators), missile strikes…nothing worked.

Yet she was sitting here on the Mirror Moon. Just her.

Her and the blond-haired, blue-eyed RDE.

Spec Ops Marines were smarter than the average spacer and had the bodies to match their job. She'd never accepted anything less in her bed.

Unable to help herself, she turned to look at Lucius. Earth-grav muscular, and smart enough get her to the Mirror Moon—something all of command's best had never achieved.

Being a girl of action—once she knew her target (*holy vacuum, she wasn't going to think about the three wasted days they'd taken getting here*)—she kissed him.

Lucius didn't do some tentative little engineer peck. Instead he reacted like a man who'd been way ahead of her on thinking about this. He brought a heat to the kiss that threatened to match the solar burn going on mere meters below their perch.

She *really* wasn't going to think about the three wasted days.

7

Lucius had been planning to suggest that they get some sleep, but his throat had been too dry to speak. Syra's record spoke for her skills. The last three days together proved a sharpness of mind that he'd found lacking in his Earth colleagues and friends. He never played stupid to fit in—which meant he rarely had—but he'd also never been so challenged.

And the way she looked. Not just the jet black suit hugging her form, but her face had utterly captivated him. Everything showed there: the wistfulness when she discussed her mother, the heat when she disagreed with something he'd said, and that laugh that he could never quite tell if it was at him or with him, but he enjoyed every time. Those green eyes held a thousand secrets yet hid nothing of the woman within.

When she kissed him, it unleashed some built-up stockpile of emotion—forever trapped behind the cool engineer. There wasn't enough room in the Inserter to do much, but that didn't stop them from trying.

"It's like trying to do it in a sports car."

"What's a—" Syra shook her head. "Never mind." She released a seam on her suit and he forgot about sports cars. Instead he discovered the softness of the woman beneath the hard shell.

And it turned out she had more than a few ideas about what they could do with six hours inside such a small space.

8

Star registered biometric changes like none she'd ever recorded. And given their current position atop the Mirror Moon, she didn't dare open the Interwave to look up what was happening.

Instead, she set up to record it for later analysis.

She cleared a large space in her permanent file so that she could save and register the information for later analysis. Perhaps it meant—

Star missed Syra's thumb coming down on the i-Loc button until it was too late to protest.

Her world went black, taking the recorders offline along with her.

Aw, Poop!

9

Descending the collecting turret six hours later was a challenge.

She wasn't all loose and gooey —that didn't happen to Royal Delta Marines, especially not this RDM. Her on-a-mission happy smile usually only came out when she was in the thick of it, but she could feel it plastered on her face.

And her hands felt hypersensitive, as if the fingertip controls inside her suit were no longer perfectly configured to the pounding pulse she could feel right out to her extremities.

Focus! She seriously had to focus.

Sure, on his Earther pectoral muscles. She'd managed to get his suit down to his waist and— Just the memory of it made her palms sweat and her head go light.

Focus!

The constant thrust to hold the Mirror Moon in place against its too-low orbit meant they weighed only fourteen percent less than on Earth's surface. Falling off the platform would offer a rapid and fiery descent into the thick mud that Earth called an atmosphere. She'd hit atmo in five minutes moving at three kilometers per second—not her idea of healthy orbital dynamics. A few of her molecules might survive to rain down on the India Beam weapon itself. Not that it would matter.

Down the tower, she approached the next challenge carefully. According to the plans that Lucius had found, the station was mostly automated…except for a detachment of the Special Frontier Force.

Once she slipped up to the first camera, she felt much better. Their particle beam might be cutting edge, but even a first-year grunt knew enough to blur an Oticus III SecureCam.

Instead of sending a blur, she flicked on both of their suits' mirroring functionality. They now projected on the front of their suits whatever appeared behind them. There was a little compounding problem, the back of her suit picking up the front of Lucius' suit, which in turn was projecting what was behind him. It wasn't the best image, but as it was supposedly impossible that they were standing on the backside of the Mirror Moon, she'd trust to lax security.

They walked into the control room at the center of the structure to find one guard, fast asleep with her feet propped on the main panel and her mouth hanging open. She woke at the moment Syra slapped on a binder that wrapped her and her arms to the chair.

"Where are all your pals?" Syra asked, but didn't expect an answer through the heavy gag she'd shoved in during the woman's initial squawk. She shot a glob of QuickFoam on both her hands, just so that she couldn't do something tricky with her fingers.

Instead Syra turned to the monitors. Thankfully they were all labeled in Standard instead of some throwback like Hindi or English.

"Oh, you guys are making this too easy." There was a fierce game of cricket going on in one of the cargo bays.

It was only a matter of a few minutes' work to set up the routine, and mere seconds to lock down all the internal accesses and then depressurize the bay. They were Special Frontier Force, so several of them made it to their weapons.

No one made it to the emergency air masks.

"Earthers! You always go for the air first," she made a tsking noise at the idiots on the display.

"You killed them!" Lucius looked at her in horror.

Syra didn't like seeing that look on his face. *Goddamn it!* After living together in the cockpit for three days, she'd forgotten that he was a civilian. And she'd...

Double damn it!

She'd thought that just maybe she'd found someone to be with for a while. It was certain that no one had ever made her feel as good as he had— Ever! And now he looked at her...the way civilians always looked at warriors.

Well, let him become reentry burn-off.

"They're Special Frontier," she waved a hand at the

screen as the last of them died, in a final, futile reach for air. "Those guys are tough. You want them running around loose to find us and off us? Five billion dead first time they used this weapon. You want five billion and two? That would make you happier?"

10

Lucius had never had anyone spit venom at him, but he couldn't think of any other word to describe it. Her voice had climbed and climbed until it rang around the control room loud enough to hurt his ears. The gagged and trussed console operator was certainly wincing.

Syra didn't turn ugly when she was furious. Instead, her green eyes seemed to go so dark he half wondered if they'd be emerald lasers that would fry him to cinders if their visors were raised.

She spun away and focused on the console.

Her next curse was so vile that he wondered if he was going to live out the next thirty seconds.

"The duty roster shows three more than I can account for in the gym. Anything you want to tell me?" She glared at the wide-eyed console operator but made no move to ungag her.

At least it wasn't him she was mad at…in this instant of time. He bet it wouldn't last.

"Get your work done, Roodee." Nope, it hadn't lasted long. "Don't release her and don't let anyone back in except me."

Before he could speak, she was out the door with no visible weapon. Though he'd wager that she was far from unarmed.

Not only wasn't he supposed to release the console operator from her chair, he inspected the arm and leg binders and didn't know if he could. If he did it wrong, he might cut her in two. Instead, he had to lean over her to reach the controls he needed and keep apologizing for each time he bumped against her.

Bumped against her.

He'd done far more than bump against Syra Clairborne. He'd discovered a fascinating, beautiful, intelligent woman who was the most unexpected person he'd ever met. A woman that he couldn't stop thinking about.

He shifted over to the security station and set an autotracker on her signal. It was double-encrypted but it was there to see if you knew the frequency. He'd expected the corridor camera to appear blank, but there she was as plain as day. Her pass-through camouflage circuitry was shut down. Yet she moved so smoothly that she might as well have been invisible. She made no motion that drew the eye. Despite that, looking away seemed to be beyond his power.

A groan of frustration from the bound console operator finally drew his attention away.

In two hours and seventeen minutes, as they passed into Earth's shadow, he had to be ready. That wasn't a problem.

The problem was that nothing in his past or his planning had prepared him for Major Syra Clairborne.

11

S he'd cleared the bunkrooms, showers, mess hall.

"Where oh where have my three lambs gone? Where oh where can they be?" Syra sang the tune quietly to herself, having no idea where she'd learned it. She'd certainly never seen a lamb. Orbital meat was all vat-grown. Actual stock animals required far too much space and resources. She'd only had Earth beef once in her life. She'd found it tough and stringy. The taste was also wrong—almost pungent—barely related to the juicy steaks that were so readily available.

And why was she being distracted by such thoughts when she was on the hunt?

Because of that idiot civilian up in the control room?

How low was that? Syra Clairborne thinking about a man during a mission.

She forced her attention ahead. There had been several outstanding maintenance items on the duty list, but no Mirror crew had been assigned to them that she'd been able to see.

At a loss, she headed toward the cargo bay to see if someone had escaped the final trap. She almost tripped on them.

The woman lay in the corridor, badly enough battered that it was hard to tell if she was conscious. She hadn't gone down without a fight, though. One man lay nearby, with his head turned at a very unlikely angle and his eyes wide. The other man, slacks down around his ankles, was busy raping the prostrate woman.

Syra didn't hesitate. She squatted to change angle and fired a bolt out of her forearm gun. It entered through his personal exhaust port or maybe it cut a new one right next to it. His skin bulged taut for a moment as the small concussion grenade went off deep inside, somewhere between his head and his heart. His scream wasn't even formed before he died.

She kicked the man aside and checked the woman's pulse. It faded away and was gone beneath her fingertips before she could even reach into her med kit. The woman still had the remnants of Army fatigues on. The men were both dressed like civilians. She checked their pockets and came up with Indian Government Inspector badges.

Worse than civilian. Earthers!

Taking down a soldier for sport.

Maybe they thought it would be easy or fun or... who knew how it started. They'd certainly gotten more than they'd bargained for.

More than she herself had bargained for. Even after she covered the woman, Syra couldn't look away.

Lucius was not like these men. As different as could be imagined.

She'd always thought of us and them: warrior and civilian.

But Lucius had far more in common with an RDM than either of these bastards.

Lucius slid in the last command and set the firing sequence. Now it was only a matter of waiting. He checked the readout.

For another nine minutes.

He'd been sweating by the time he'd finished, trying to beat the launch deadline had been tighter than he'd thought. His information was old and there'd been several systems upgrades since then. It had required reprogramming several of his canned routines.

For two hours he'd been working around and over the silent console operator. She'd slowly shifted from wide-eyed fear to giving him a nod in the right direction when he couldn't find a control. The gag had also been outside his experience and he'd apologized when he told her that they'd both be better off if he didn't touch it.

Eight minutes. He stretched his aching muscles.

That meant—

"Syra!" Gone for over two hours. Was she dead?

He spun to the door to race into the halls and find her.

But there she was, sitting on the floor with her back against the door, watching him.

"Thank god!" She didn't respond. Syra simply sat and looked at him with no expression for the longest time before she spoke.

"You a believer?"

Lucius had to think for a moment before he realized that she was responding to his own exclamation.

The Middle East Faceoff had been merely bloody until it went nuclear and then it was thoroughly devastating. Religion hadn't been real popular after the decade-long nuclear winter that the conflict had caused. The Vatican was the only major religious center politically savvy enough to stay out of the fray, but a gang of renegade Episcopalians had taken them down shortly afterward. Nobody had seemed to care by that point.

"No," Lucius shook his head. "Not really. I believe in people."

"Are you demented?"

He shook his head.

"How can you accept…" she waved a hand toward something in another section of the Mirror Moon, but then let her hand drop. It was as if someone had drained the life out of her. It was just wrong to see her like this. He stepped over to squat down in front of her until they were eye-to-eye.

"It's easy, Syra. Look at where you got us on this

mission. You made hard decisions that I never could, but they were good ones."

"Were they?"

"We're here. We're alive. It's the cruelty of governments that baffle me, because somehow it overshadows the good deeds of people."

"Not all people," there were dark shadows deep in those green eyes.

He shrugged. "I've met the bad ones, too."

"What do you do?"

"I don't kill them."

Her scowl said that he'd just put his foot in it. And in the past it was the sort of thing he'd have done. But he understood Syra better now. He understood the terror of the machine he'd just sabotaged and that it had to be stopped at any cost.

So, instead of stammering, apologizing, or wondering what to do about his lousy choice of words, he sat down beside her, leaned back against the door, and took her hand in his.

"I'm not saying that sometimes they don't need to be killed. I've been thinking about that a lot over these last hours."

"I thought you were busy programming."

"I was multitasking." He smiled across at her, glad that she'd retracted her helmet back into the suit. "I'm saying that killing is something I don't do. It's not my skill. I may hate its necessity, but you're right. All those billions. A few more to avert a darker future is a good thing."

"So I'm the killer. What do you do?"

He glanced at his timepiece. "This. I do this." He slid a hand around her waist.

The program launched.

With a stomach-wrenching lurch, the room flipped on its back. He hooked a table leg with one hand and held them both in place. Her suit might be hard on the outside. In fact, he suspected that's how everyone saw her, including herself—hard and strong through and through. But he'd seen the sadness in her eyes and knew there was so much more to Major Syra Clairborne than medals and bravado.

He kissed her as the room lurched into its new position. He wasn't sure if the nervous flip in his stomach was due to the room or the kiss.

"What just happened?" And Syra's tone said that she wasn't sure which she was reacting to either.

"I flipped the station on edge. Just as we entered Earth shadow. Now neither reflector is facing India, but the solar collector is perfectly aimed to get maximum efficiency from the sun. It should take them a while to figure out that they can no longer see the Mirror Moon by which time we'll be in a very different orbit." He'd been counting seconds in the back of his mind as he spoke. "And…now!"

The station jolted hard and the floor was once again the floor.

"I just fired all of the orbit-keeping engines, except now they're facing along Earth's orbit instead of straight down. We're firing them on full and diving down close to the atmosphere until we gain speed. Enough speed to break out of orbit."

"Leaving Earth. Where are we going? You never said."

"I'm going to park it in the one place that India can't see."

Syra blinked. Twice. But not a third time. Then she started laughing.

The captive still strapped in her chair on the far side of the room was barely slower, barking out a hoarse sound of surprise around the gag. Her eyes were laughing—saying that maybe she wouldn't mind never going back to India—and that tipped Syra right over the edge.

Her own laugh shook her right down to the core. It might have been tears for a moment. For the woman who had died in the corridor. For the one bound and gagged but now aglow with the fresh energy of hope. For all those who had died in all of these pointless wars.

But at the core, it was still a laugh and that finally triumphed like it was purging her soul. When she could catch her breath, she answered her own question.

"You're parking it out at L2 with the British habitat cans, hiding it behind Lunar Farside. We're going to the asshole of space."

Lucius nodded. "We'll be out of range of the particle beam in another twenty-seven minutes. That's all we need for them to not pay attention."

"And if they're paying attention?"

Lucius shrugged.

And Syra knew. Just because he was an engineer who didn't kill people, didn't mean that he was a man controlled by fear any more than a Marine. For twenty-seven more minutes he had accepted that they might be killed. With the reflector turned to the side, the India Beam would blast through the habitat-and-control structure mounted between the beam-reflecting mirror and the solar power-collecting one. He'd accepted the risk of death to solve the problem. Definitely her kind of man.

"Once it's there at L2," Lucius continued as if it was a certainty. "It will be a secondary light source for Farside. I'll configure the reflector to gather the sun and shine it back down on the surface. The two weeks of darkness out of every Lunar month shall now become both light and a source of energy."

It was so out of the box. It was like a brilliant military maneuver that there was no way to understand until it had been completed.

Farside hadn't been properly set up before the Earth failures began happening. It was safe there, but the struggles to stabilize the colonies were ongoing. Having power and light shine down from the Mirror Moon rather than being trapped in the long Lunar night was going to help the tens of millions fighting to survive there.

"You did that," she could only whisper in awe.

He shrugged easily enough, but his smile was at least a little smug—pride of ownership smug. There was modest and then there was stupid, and Roodee Lucius Markham wasn't stupid.

"I thought it up the first time I saw it as a kid. I haven't done anything else for the last decade except figure out how to make this happen."

"And you did."

"And I did."

Syra thought about that. It was a personal drive of perseverance worthy of a Clairborne woman. Down a different path, but no less important.

"How long will it take to get there?"

"Six days." He checked his timepiece. "And twenty-four minutes."

She still had to interrogate and consider freeing the prisoner. Make sure the security systems were fully under their control and that no booby traps were waiting. But that wasn't going to take six days. It would probably take less than one.

"Six days and twenty-four minutes?"

"Twenty-three now."

"You *are* an engineer."

Lucius combined a nod with a shrug of those nice shoulders.

"I can think of a lot that we can do with six days." Her voice was whispery and happy in a way she barely recognized.

"I hope they're the same things that I'm thinking of."

Syra couldn't help but smile at the tone in his voice. "Let's just say that they're probably along the same mission profile."

"Good." Lucius kissed her on the temple.

She leaned into it and marveled at how good it felt. It wasn't a kiss of a good sexual romp, that was already a given.

No. It was a promise of so much more if she was

willing. Time would tell, but once a Clairborne woman found her man, she kept him for good—just like Dad and Grandpop.

"What color is your hair?" His whisper tickled her ear.

"Same as Mom and Grandmom's."

He snorted a laugh. "Helpful."

"Just the kind of woman I am. It's even more regressive than your blond."

"Red," he said it like a gasp of wonder. "Red hair and green eyes."

Which was exactly why she kept it shaved. Men always got all weird about red hair because it was so rare. But this time he'd already been on board before he found out.

"If you're a very good boy, I might even grow it out for you."

His kiss said that he wasn't too good a boy. It was a very nice kiss.

She relaxed into it and let it slowly warm her body. Let it heat and melt that dark core she'd always held so close to her heart.

Lucius was bringing light to half a world.

And he was also giving it to her and she knew it would shine for a lifetime.

If you liked this, you'll love:
The Nara Reaction

(excerpt follows).
And we love getting reviews, too!

THE NARA REACTION

(EXCERPT)

SPACE ADVENTURE AT ITS FINEST

"**S**o, I'm dead, am I?"

It was perfect. James Wirden's voice started with all the power one would expect from the World Premier, but it ended the most delicious twist of uncertainty. Bryce looked down at the nearly empty champagne glass in James' hand.

"Yes, sad for you, but true. Poisoned, if you must know. By me."

"And you dare to tell me this?" Such indignation from such a small man. He turned toward the guards, but Bryce clamped a friendly hand upon his shoulder to belay the movement. Not that it mattered, all of the guards along the line of French doors were his hand-picked staff. The bright lights from within cast their tall shadows across the stone terrace pushing back the edge of the Bermudan night. His men would stop any stragglers from the party, not that any would dare interrupt when the Premier and his mighty right-hand man were in conference. But no point in misplacing trust when one staged a coup.

"One of the many things you never properly appreciated, James, is the wonders of modern genetics. There is a tiny little code-alterer running through your system even as we speak. Your genetic code is even now shifting at an exquisitely subtle level. When you have a massive stroke in three days, none shall grieve as much as your lieutenant. None shall take power with as much trepidation as your Right Hand." A nickname Bryce had carefully cultivated for years. Who better to be named to power than the man who knew the Premier's every intent?

The man struggled against his grasp just as pointlessly as a worm evading a short future pithed upon the hook that would send it into the fish's belly. Bryce took the champagne glass from James' nerveless hand and tipped the dregs over the broad stone seawall to splash into the eager waves below. Soon, he promised them, soon you may swallow this useless chattel as well.

The Premier's pale face twisted in such pain that for a moment Bryce feared the stroke would come too soon. He didn't have everything in place yet. Of course, he could compensate, but having the man die in his arms would not look good at all to the World Economic Council.

"You must remember to breathe, my good leader. Besides, in another few minutes you will remember none of this. Another wonder of genetics research you so despise is the revelation of how memories are stored. Your memory of these moments will shortly be erased. And when you pass on in three day's time, your Right Hand will be there, the Premier-to-be, Bryce Randall Stevens, Sr."

James patted at the beads of sweat on his brow with his small hand as he looked up at Bryce. He always backed up when they spoke so that he didn't have to crane his neck, but Bryce kept him in his place this time. The music surged through the open doors onto the broad patio. The orchestra had come back precisely on schedule drawing everyone's attention inward. He didn't want any to think his conversation with the Premier took overlong if the drug didn't take effect as planned. Of course he knew it would, it had worked perfectly on the man who'd engineered it for him.

"Do you hate me so?"

"Stupid man, what does hate have to do with anything? You're weak, James. Always were. If I hadn't pulled every single string over the last four decades, Parvati and her temple of democratic fairness would still be in power. I have used you, because you are far more presentable than I. No one expects a small, rotund man to be vicious. Therefore, there were no curious eyes as I did what you were too weak to do behind the scenes. But now you are beginning to interfere. You should never have nuked Auckland."

The little man sputtered. "I had to Bryce. You and your damned gene labs. There is a reason we outlawed that horrible knowledge. We did it. You and I. Together.

When I found you were dabbling in that dark road to hell, of course I had to blow it out of existence."

"Too little, too late, James. Do you think I'd have let you drop those bombs if I wasn't ready? All you did for me was a little convenient housecleaning." Actually he'd barely gotten the chief scientists and the data clear. Less than an hour warning had let him salvage only the most essential elements. But the continuing research on the uses of the Second Human Genome Mapping Project lived on, even if the researchers families hadn't. And he'd gotten to look like the hero to the ones he had saved.

The blow of his failure took the fight out of the Premier. Bryce gave James' shoulder a jovial shake in show for any who might be watching.

"On December 24th, three days after this birthday party, lovingly thrown by your second-in-command, I shall mourn at your side. I shall cancel Christmas throughout the planet. It shall be a splendid funeral. And by the New Year, the World Economic Council will place me in command and then things shall really start to move."

James' little eyes squinted up at him for a long moment before turning to look out at the restless sea. He hung onto the rough seawall to keep from being toppled by the gentle night breeze and stared toward the dark waves.

"They will suspect you."

"There will be no proof. The last of the drug has just been dribbled into the sea. The change to your genetic code has already been registered in your electronic medical records, by a fine hacker who has, alas, suffered a memory loss due to some bad fish he ate. Very bad fish. You don't maintain paper files, so I'm safe."

Bryce leaned down to watch his face, but James was turned toward the night and he was totally in shadow. There was a long hesitation, then a twitch of his shoulders that Bryce could feel beneath his hand.

"But I do. I was most careful."

Not careful enough, old friend. He knew when James' was lying. It was for this that Bryce had risked telling him of his own death. The man was so naive that he hadn't banked hard copies against his future. So, Bryce's plan was going to go off without a hitch.

The Premier hung his head and his voice was a mere whisper against the susurration of the surf on the rocky cliffs below.

"What about my wife?"

Bryce glanced back to the surging dance floor. What an odd final question to ask before certain death. Given a chance, what would be his last request? Not about some woman, that was for certain. Though if ever there was one...

Even through the crowd Celia Wirden stood out. Her fountain of white-blond hair and the slender body beneath, shimmeringly not revealed by her gown of midnight-blue silk, did everything to distract from the brilliant mind that hid behind those green eyes.

The three of them had plotted together since they were young. They had thrown Parvati out of power and when it came time to choose, Bryce had forced the milquetoast James to puppet the Premiership for him. And the Premier needed a First Lady. A fine and elegant First Lady she had made. Perhaps it was time to take that gift back.

"She'll be taken care of, James. You don't need to fear for that."

James' shoulders squared slowly as the man looked a last time at the dark Atlantic. He took up his empty champagne glass from the seawall.

"Well, old friend. Seems that I am dry. Shall we go get a refill?"

"I am right beside you to the end of your days, James."

"Long may that be."

Bryce completed their old code, "Long indeed."

At the French doors, he checked James one last time. But he was filled with a bonhomie that even the finest politician couldn't invent. When he refilled the same glass and drank from it, Bryce knew the memory of the last few minutes was safely gone.

James was wrapped up into the flow of the crowd as Bryce waited upon the threshold. The broad squares of alternating black and white marble spread across the room before him like a grand chess board. The sycophants rushed to make what they could of the moment, shuffling like mad pawns, the tuxedoed livery of the government descended upon the wrong man. The short stature of the largest pawn of them all disappeared from view. Bryce would keep a close eye upon him, but not too close. Nothing must seem out of the ordinary.

He scanned the room. The ladies, those dragged forward by their men, and those abandoned in the sudden rush toward the Premier, glittered about. Their 1920s flapper costumes revealing both the wondrous and the corpulent with an equal lack of sympathy. But they too were all either carefully watching the rush to the Premier, or carefully not watching.

There were just four who were watching the Premier's Right Hand instead. His Captain of the guard, meticulous in his waiter's outfit, was nonchalantly poised to strike from his corner like a steadfast rook. The general commander of the World Economic Council's forces waited like the good knight he was, not obviously aligned, yet always prepared to offer surprise support from unexpected quarters.

Celia Wirden glittered like the queen that she was. The tight silk revealed a mature woman who had grown into her body the way a yacht grows into a World Cup racer. Her movements could light fire without ever striking a match.

His body responded from the memory of that one tryst three decades gone, the same night he'd sent her to become James' first lady. Her green eyes assessed him carefully from her position far across the room near the small orchestra. A chandelier blossomed above her in a font of crystal as if it had bloomed for her alone.

And off to the side, behind the piano, hid a single junior pawn. Without even the boy being aware, Bryce had been moving him across the board, square by careful square. Perhaps it was time to move the lad one step closer to the far side of the board, where he too would become powerful. Together, many things could be achieved. Bryce would kill the king, take the queen, and create a prince.

Yes. It was time for the next move.

Keep reading at fine retailers everywhere.

ABOUT THE AUTHOR

M.L. Buchman started the first of over 50 novels and even more short stories while flying from South Korea to ride across the Australian Outback. All part of a solo around-the-world bicycle trip (a mid-life crisis on wheels) that ultimately launched his writing career.

Booklist has selected his military and firefighter series(es) as 3-time "Top 10 Romance of the Year." NPR and Barnes & Noble have named other titles "Top 5 Romance of the Year." In 2016 he was a finalist for RWA's RITA award.

He has flown and jumped out of airplanes, can single-hand a fifty-foot sailboat, and has designed and built two houses. In between writing, he also quilts. M.L. is constantly amazed at what can be done with a degree in geophysics. He also writes: contemporary romance, thrillers, and SF. More info at: www.mlbuchman.com

Join the conversation:
www.mlbuchman.com

Other works by M. L. Buchman:

The Night Stalkers

MAIN FLIGHT
The Night Is Mine
I Own the Dawn
Wait Until Dark
Take Over at Midnight
Light Up the Night
Bring On the Dusk
By Break of Day

WHITE HOUSE HOLIDAY
Daniel's Christmas
Frank's Independence Day
Peter's Christmas
Zachary's Christmas
Roy's Independence Day
Damien's Christmas

AND THE NAVY
Christmas at Steel Beach
Christmas at Peleliu Cove

5E
Target of the Heart
Target Lock on Love
Target of Mine

Firehawks

MAIN FLIGHT
Pure Heat
Full Blaze
Hot Point
Flash of Fire
Wild Fire

SMOKEJUMPERS
Wildfire at Dawn
Wildfire at Larch Creek
Wildfire on the Skagit

Delta Force
Target Engaged
Heart Strike
Wild Justice

White House Protection Force
Off the Leash
On Your Mark
In the Weeds

Where Dreams
Where Dreams are Born
Where Dreams Reside
Where Dreams Are of Christmas
Where Dreams Unfold
Where Dreams Are Written

Eagle Cove
Return to Eagle Cove
Recipe for Eagle Cove
Longing for Eagle Cove
Keepsake for Eagle Cove

Henderson's Ranch
Nathan's Big Sky
Big Sky, Loyal Heart

Love Abroad
Heart of the Cotswolds: England
Path of Love: Cinque Terre, Italy

Dead Chef Thrillers
Swap Out!
One Chef!
Two Chef!

Deities Anonymous
Cookbook from Hell: Reheated
Saviors 101

SF/F Titles
The Nara Reaction
Monk's Maze
the Me and Elsie Chronicles

Strategies for Success (NF)
Managing Your Inner Artist/Writer
Estate Planning for Authors